Piglet and Granny

by Margaret Wild

illustrated by

Stephen Michael King

ABRAMS BOOKS FOR YOUNG READERS

NEW YORK

For Sandy Campbell, with love —M.W.

For Nana —S.M.K.

Stephen Michael King used watercolor and black ink for the illustrations in this book.

Library of Congress Cataloging-in-Publication Data

Wild, Margaret, 1948–
Piglet and Granny / by Margaret Wild ; illustrated by Stephen Michael King.
p. cm.
Summary: While Piglet waits for her fun-loving Granny to visit, she impresses the other farm animals with some of
the skills she has taught her, such as balancing and turning somersaults.
ISBN 978-0-8109-4063-5
[1. Grandmothers—Fiction. 2. Pigs—Fiction. 3. Domestic animals—Fiction. 4. Farm life—Fiction.] I. King, Stephen
Michael, ill. II. Title.

PZ7.W64574Ph 2009
[E]—dc22
2008046400

Text copyright © 2009 Margaret Wild
Illustrations copyright © 2009 Stephen Michael King
Book design by Melissa Arnst

Printed and bound in China
10 9 8 7 6 5 4 3 2 1

Abrams Books for Young Readers are available at special discounts when purchased in quantity for premiums and
promotions as well as fundraising or educational use. Special editions can also be created to specification. For
details, contact specialmarkets@hnabooks.com or the address below.

HNA
harry n. abrams, inc.
a subsidiary of La Martinière Groupe
115 West 18th Street
New York, NY 10011
www.hnabooks.com

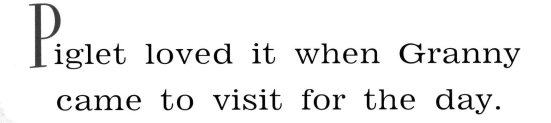

Piglet loved it when Granny
came to visit for the day.

Although Granny
was soft and squishy,
she was as lively as a
family of leaping frogs.
And she had such good
ideas for things to do.

One morning, Piglet waited by
the gate for Granny to arrive.

She waited and waited.
But Granny didn't come.

Piglet wobbled along the wall,
trying to keep her balance.

"What good balancing!"
said Cow.

"My granny taught me,"
said Piglet. "I'm waiting
for her to visit."

"I'm sure she'll be along soon,"
said Cow.

But Granny didn't come.

Piglet chased after some butterflies.

"What fast running!" said Horse.

"My granny taught me," said Piglet.
"I'm waiting for her to visit."

"I'm sure she won't be too long,"
said Horse.

But Granny didn't come.

Piglet

    did

        somersaults

            down

                the

                    slope.

"What amazing somersaults!"
said Duck.

"My granny taught me," said Piglet.
"I'm waiting for her to visit."

"I'm sure she'll be here any moment," said Duck.

But Granny didn't come.

Piglet played hide-and-seek in
the long grass.

"What a clever hiding place!"
said Sheep.

"My granny taught me," said Piglet.
"I'm waiting for her to visit."

"I've been waiting

 and waiting

and waiting!"

"I'm sure she'll come
as soon as she can,"
said Sheep, giving Piglet a cuddle.

Piglet swung on the gate.

Back and forth.

Back and forth.

Squeak.

Squeak.

Squeak.

Behind her, a voice said,
"May I swing, too?"

"Granny!" said Piglet.

"I'm sorry I'm late," said Granny, "but I was making a surprise for you."

"A surprise?" said Piglet. "What is it?"

"Come down to the stream with me," said Granny, "and you'll find out."

On the way to the stream, Piglet tried to guess what the surprise was.

"Are we going to paddle?"

"Are we going to float sticks?"

"Are we going to look for tadpoles?"

But Granny just smiled
and shook her head.

Then they were at the stream—

—and there was the surprise!

A slippery, slithery mudslide!

Piglet and Granny
slid and swooshed

again

and

again

and

again

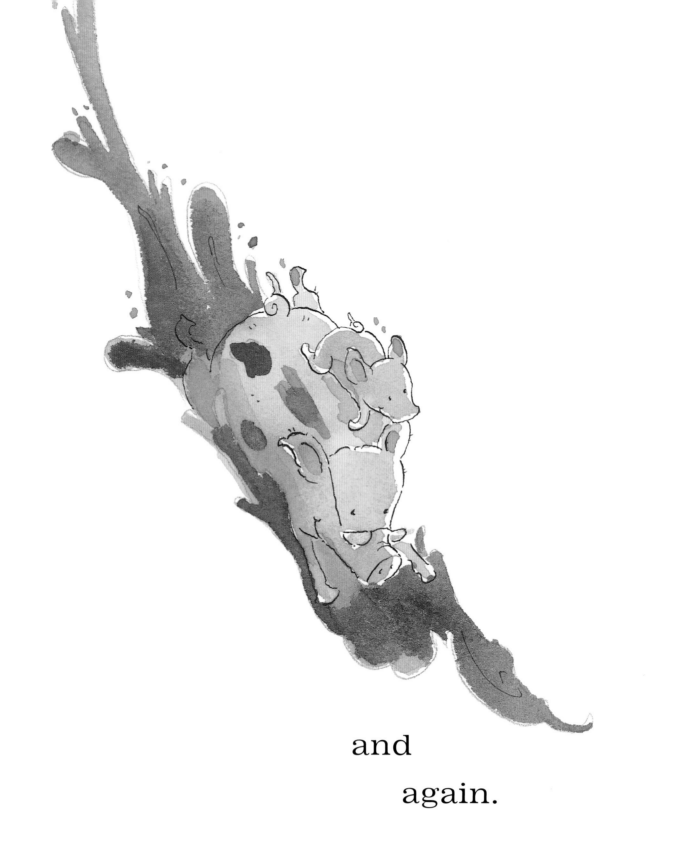

and
again.

"I like it when you visit, Granny,"
said Piglet.

"And I love being here with you," said
Granny, "best piglet in all the world!"

And together they went

for one last

SPLASHY

slide!